WINSTON
the
TRAVELING
DOG

by Cynthia Anne Finefrock

Faithful Friends Publishing

ISBN 978-1-7369459-0-2

First Edition

CynthiaAnne.com

This book belongs to

_____

and is a gift from

_____

This is Winston - a furry and energetic Pomeranian from the USA. Winston lives a great life and has no complaints! Well... except maybe that he isn't allowed to eat at the dinner table with the rest of his family. And, I guess while we're on that topic, he would also like to have free access to the refrigerator. He's a growing boy, after all.

travel channel

There's a whole world out there!

Anyway, back to the story. It all began one day when Winston started feeling as though something was missing in his life. He couldn't quite put his paw on what it was. That is, until he was watching the Travel Channel and realized he hadn't ever strayed farther than his own backyard. It turned out, there was a whole world out there - and now he was determined to see it.

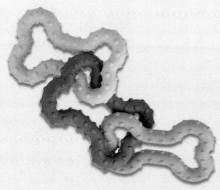

After getting approval from his pawrents, Winston packed his chew toys, a few bones, and a paper map in his backpack. "Adventure, here I come!" barked Winston.

On the plane, Winston thought about his upcoming adventures. He was a little nervous to go somewhere he had never been before. Despite being scared, he reminded himself that venturing outside of what feels comfortable would make him a stronger, more confident Pom.

Winston's first stop was London. After arriving there, Winston started the day at Buckingham Palace. Winston tried numerous approaches to make the guards laugh, but no amount of sniffing, pawing or barking could do the trick.

While viewing the London Eye, Winston worked up quite an appetite.

After finishing fish and chips for lunch and a treacle tart for dessert, Winston ended the day with a stroll through Green Park and past Tower Bridge. "London is so much fun! I don't know how the rest of my trip is going to top this!" barked Winston.

The next morning, Winston took a train to Paris.

LONDON · PARIS

UNITED KINGDOM
LONDON

Winston's first stop in Paris was shopping along the Champs-Élysées. He bought a striped sweater and a fancy red scarf — *très chic!* Wearing his new clothes and feeling like a true Parisian, he took a long walk past the Arc de Triomphe and the Eiffel Tower.

While drooling over the Eiffel Tower, he spotted the most beautiful
chihuahua he had ever seen. Winston decided to say hello in French.
"Bonjour! Would you like to share a macaron and a puppuccino with
me?" Winston asked the chihuahua. Lucky for Winston, she thought his
outfit was cute and quickly said yes, or "oui," as they say in French.

Italy

Venice

Milan

Rome

Sardinia

Sicily

After an amazing afternoon, Winston reluctantly said goodbye to his new friend. He was sad to leave Paris, but excited to keep exploring Europe. Next stop: Italy!

Winston was a little disappointed to learn it's the Leaning Tower of *Pisa*, not the Leaning Tower of *Pizza*.

Buon Appetito

Speaking of pizza...

The rest of Winston's Italian adventures consisted of visiting the Duomo in Florence, making a wish at Trevi Fountain in Rome, and attempting to find George Clooney's house in Lake Como. (George Clooney is Winston's favorite movie star and he had heard he lived somewhere around there.)

ITALY
Florence Cathedral

ciao

ROME

At last, Winston's travels came to an end. Reflecting on his time abroad, Winston couldn't decide what his favorite part of the trip had been. Maybe it was practicing other languages or trying new cuisines. Or, quite possibly, it was meeting a new friend that he wouldn't have otherwise met. In any case, Winston promised himself he would keep traveling and exploring the big world around him as much as he could. Anything is pawsible, if you put your mind to it.

The End

(until next time ...)

Cynthia Anne Finefrock lives in Scottsdale, Arizona with her furry roommates, Winston and Sparrow.

Before she ventured into the world of writing, Cynthia graduated from the University of Southern California before obtaining her Masters in Physician Assistant Studies from Cornell University. Academics aside, Cynthia's true passion is experiencing as much of the world as possible through the lens of her camera. After designing a website to showcase her diverse photography, Cynthia decided to edit her dog Winston into her travel landscapes. What started as a comical exchange between friends has transpired into a published book.

If you would like to stay updated on Winston's fabulous life, please follow him on Instagram @WinstonTravels_. You can also visit CynthiaAnne.com for updates on potential new releases. Winston still has a lot of traveling to do, after all...